KWABENA AND THE MAGIC RIVER

PART 1

DAWN BAABA ARTHUR

ISBN: 978-0-9567068-0-5

Illustrations by **Daniel Ofosu**

Edited by **Betty-Ann Biggart**

Printed by supreme**printers.**com +44 (0)20 7249 9211

ACKNOWLEDGEMENT

In this life, no one walks alone and many people come and offer help in many ways but permit me to make special mention of certain people whose immense help and support has undeniably helped in the successful writing of this book.

First and foremost, I thank my God and Saviour. Without Him I am nothing and with Him all things including this book are possible. I bless His Holy Name.

A special thanks and gratitude to Miss Gloria McDonald, who never gave up on me, Mrs. Elizabeth Mensah, Miss Georgia McDowe, Miss Florence Kusi-Appiah, and Miss Love Arthur who have always provided shoulders to lean on and whose words of wisdom and encouragement, have helped me throughout the years.

I must not forget to thank my children and grandchildren who in their own ways inspired me and blessed me with their faithful Love and support. Thank you kids for being patient with my late nights while writing this book.

I also have to thank Daniel Ofosu, my illustrator with an abundance of talent who skillfully captures my words into art. Good work! And my editor Betty-Ann Biggart, thank you.

Thank you to everyone who will buy and read this book.

FOREWORD

The opening statement made by the author in the Acknowledgment is an apt summary of the story in The Magic River. She magnificently juxtaposes the traditional against the scientific, the rural to the urban, and the old to the new.

Story-telling is a craft, an art, and in most Ghanaian societies the evenings are times for story-telling. In the story-telling sessions human emotions and frailties come to the fore.

A good story teller does not only create laughter, occasionally they invoke other attitudes such as anger or pity from their audiences and Dawn has successfully demonstrated this in the 'The Magic River'.

Tim. E. Andoh [University of Ghana, Legon]

Synopsis:

KWABENA AND THE MAGIC RIVER

Though this story looks at the poverty of a family in a small closely-knit village in Ghana, the events which follow will take them to far away Canada to make a better life for themselves.

The people in the village treat each other like family members, so when the entire Banquo family disappear after going to fetch water along the river, it is not surprising how badly affected they were.

The fortunes of this family change when they realise that the river holds supernatural and magical powers which could change their lives for good.

Faith, courage and steadfast determination personify the character of Kwabena Banquo, whose perseverance brings good fortune to his family.

The characters and places mentioned in this book are fictional and any resemblance with real life names are purely coincidental.

CHAPTER 1

In the heart of a village called Banhoff, lived a man and his three sons. Long before the death of his wife, he became the enemy of the entire village. He was known for being mean and wicked. His wife, however, was able to foster some good relationships with some of the villagers so nobody bothered much about the man anymore. His sons too did not get on well with their peers. Very often, the villagers would gather under the neem tree to play different kinds of games. In Ghana, the neem tree has been said to possess medicinal properties to cure fever and jaundice. There was never a time when Mr. Banquo would come out of his hut to share his views with the other elders of the village. They came out to sit together on benches when the moon emerged, to discuss the welfare of the village and their own personal problems.

The children would also gather to sing, run about and play games like "Hide and Seek" and Ampe. Ampe is a clapping and jumping game played by two or more people. It is about predicting and mirroring the leader's movement. If the movements of two people correspond at a time, they both gain a point. If one does not correspond, they lose a point, so the children in the village had fun playing this game.

Mr Banquo owned a very big farm; in the farm were fruits like mangoes, guava, coconut, oranges and other citrus fruits. They were sweet and tasty. He often sold his products at nearby villages or he boarded one of the only two Lorries which travelled between the village and the city, about 100

miles away. He normally carried the load in baskets or sacks with his family to sell in the market. If he found anyone wandering in his farm, he dealt with them severely. It seems after his wife died he became worse than before. He was once accused of plucking a young boy down from the top of an orange tree and chasing him off of his property.

CHAPTER 2

One fine evening, Mr. Banquo and his three sons Josef, Kojo, and Kwabena went to the nearby stream to fetch water. It was quarter of a mile away. On reaching there, they discovered to their surprise that the stream had completely dried up, and that was something which was unheard of.

The river had never dried up before. Just as they were wondering what to do next, darkness suddenly began to appear and a strong wind blew over the area. Panic and fear gripped them. In an instant, a very huge creature appeared. It wobbled with five legs, talked with three heads and peered at them through ten eyes. Josef the eldest son shouted to his father and brothers to run from it but they couldn't find their way out since the whole place had become completely dark. Before they knew it, the monster had already swallowed them up and like a dream; they ended up in an unbelievable scientific world.

Everything in there was operated by the touch of a button. The boys thought they had been taken to heaven. "Could this be the so called Heaven that is always preached to us any time we go to church?" asked Kojo the second born. His father, Mr Banquo was frozen with fear so he did not answer him. Then from nowhere appeared this beautiful woman dressed in sparkling gold standing in front of them. Mr. Banquo was luckily saved from collapsing on the floor by his children who firmly held him.

Only heavens know what would have happened if the

woman had touched Mr. Banquo. Kwabena, the last-born told his father to gather courage, as his legs were shaking like the drill they had seen the workmen using on the road.

The lady's dress was glittering as she kept staring at them in silence. Meanwhile, the boys tried to compose themselves but Josef suddenly clenched his stomach. He felt hungry since he had not had anything to eat that day.

In fact, they were going to fetch the water to prepare something to eat after a long day at the farm.

The lady in gold pushed a button and out came a table from the wall full of assorted foods. A voice instructed them to sit beside the table. Different kinds of drinks were also assembled on the table. All this time, Mr Banquo was staring at the woman in awe. The woman sat down and also invited the four strangers to sit as well. She beckoned them to eat.

Since they were not used to eating with cutlery, they didn't know whether to eat with their hands or use the cutlery to impress their hostess.

Mr. Banquo was the first to pick up his set of cutlery, but his trembling hands dropped them and the boys teased and laughed at him.

CHAPTER 3

Back in Banhoff, the villagers grew worried about the whereabouts of the Banquo family who by this time had not been seen for two days. What alarmed them most was that someone had spotted their buckets by the stream, so fears grew that some wild animals might have killed them.

The town crier, a man who conveys messages from the palace to the villagers, was ordered by the chief to beat the gong-gong and a search party was organised to look for them.

For about one week, there wasn't any trace of them. The question of them being drowned was completely out of the question because River Selbs, the local stream was not big or deep enough to drown people. Fetish priests and local magic men from around the area were called to help find them but their special magic powers were unsuccessful in determining the whereabouts of the Banquos. Fear gripped the entire village and its surroundings. Could it be that a bad omen was about to befall them or was it just a matter of accidental death to the family?

Months went by and nothing was heard of them so they were presumed dead. You can imagine the zeal and anxiety with which the children frequented Mr Banquo's farm for fruits. Some of the children were afraid that Mr. Banquo's ghost would come and haunt them so they dared not go there at all. However, among some of them, it became a matter of "Who dares wins," so they took the chance to help themselves. People would often gather to discuss the mysterious disappearance of the Banquo family but nobody ever wanted to walk alone, for fear of being a victim of this tragedy.

Mr. Banquo and his children were gradually coming to terms with their new home. The children showed more courage than their father did. If it was possible for him to turn himself into an ant to escape, he would have done so. He was always thinking about his house and the farms. The farms were now turning into thick bushes and his house was being swallowed by weeds. Because of his wickedness, nobody even bothered to sweep the surroundings of the house to kill off the weeds. Moreover, they didn't even know what might have happened to him. It could be that he was dead and his ghost was hovering around his house.

CHAPTER 4

Life at this new place was quite simple and enjoyable for the boys. There was no such thing as going to the farm to clear the bushes or going to draw water from the stream in this place. Nobody will even tell them to go out and buy soap from the corner shop. They had absolute freedom. The only thing they missed most was their friends. Their makeshift wooden beds in the village were now a thing of the past, with their never to be forgotten hard mattresses infected with bedbugs. In fact, mere words cannot describe their old furnishings and their muddy red walkways in the village.

For all these months, the villagers were still full of fear and talking about the mysterious disappearance of the Banquo family.

One day, a man, his wife and their three daughters from the same village of Banhoff went to the farm for foodstuffs. On their way back, their eight year old daughter Aisha spotted a very beautiful bird lying on the bank of the river. "Mummy, Mummy, can I take it home and nurse it?" asked the little girl.

"No," was the sharp

reply from her mum. However, she defied her mother and took the bird home; she put it beside the fire for it to get a little bit of warmth. In the night, she kept it in an old cage and went to sleep. Aisha was thinking about the bird so much that she could not sleep. She was the first person to wake up the next "What happened?" she thought, "How could the bird have escaped?" "Where did it go?"

She ran, screaming to her mother, who was still asleep. Her thoughts were that her mother might have sent it away in the night. Her noise woke everyone up. The eldest sister Ama accused her of making an unnecessary racket. No amount of explanation would calm her down, so she decided to go and look for the bird herself. She went to look in the old cage where she kept the bird to see if it had come back but instead of the wounded bird, she saw a glittering stone in the cage. Her family thought the bird might have turned

itself into the stone, which sparked another fear that something evil was about to happen but they could not be sure.

The whole village came to have a glimpse of the 'bird which had turned into a stone' and they advised the family to go back to the bush and throw it away but how could they throw such a beautiful thing away?

Some people thought it could be that an old ancestor was bringing them riches since they have been in poverty for years. However, the little girl was still convinced that the bird had been thrown away into the bush so she decided to go to the bush and look for it. Advice from her parents and some elderly people in the village did not remove her heartache. She went to the river side where she first found the bird and sat there crying.

After a while, darkness was falling and the girl had not returned. Her father panicked and decided to go out to look for her; he combed the whole place, occasionally calling her name but there was no sign of her. He went round in circles looking for his daughter but he could not find her. He went back to the river side one more time to see if the girl was there but she wasn't. Just as her father turned to leave, he spotted an envelope lying near the river bank, the very spot where they had seen the wounded bird.

He contemplated leaving it but something moved his heart to pick it up. He went back to the village and straight to the village teacher's house. The village teacher would read it for him since he was illiterate. The note apparently had been written by the river.

According to the letter, the river had taken the little girl and the Banquo family. This was in retaliation for the persistent abuse of the river by the villagers who were fond of throwing rubbish and washing dirty things in it. The river therefore instructed the king and fetish priest to perform some rituals to pacify the river in return for the missing villagers and to swear an oath that nothing of the sort would happen again.

CHAPTER 5

Meanwhile, Aisha really felt at home in the company of Mr Banquo and his sons. The little girl told them that everyone in the village had feared for their safety and presumed they were dead. However, they accepted life as it was in this remarkable place and enjoyed it. They didn't have the slightest idea that one day; they would go back to the village to see the old folks again. To them, it was like reincarnation, until one day, the beautiful lady came to tell them that the whole village was grieving over them, so they should be going back.

She said all the necessary rituals had been performed for their return so they had to go. They received the news with mixed feelings. "So we are going back into poverty again"? asked Josef. "Oh no!" exclaimed the youngest son.

In fact, the thought of going back to clear the bushes and the difficult manual work awaiting them sickened the kids. Over here they did nothing. They only had to wake up from bed, have a shower, eat and play as many games as they wanted.

One full moon, as the villagers were getting ready for their usual gathering, Akosua, the daughter of the village crier, ran hysterically to the Chief's palace. She had gone to fetch water from the river and met a stunning lady who gave her a message for the chief. The lady had asked Akosua to tell the chief that at long last Mr. Banquo and his three sons and Aisha were finally coming back home. The news swept across the village like a hurricane wind. Everybody wanted to catch a glimpse of the missing people.

On the day of their arrival, the king ordered the gong-gong beaters to beat the gong gong and inform the whole village of an important meeting at the palace. Since the palace was not big enough, sheds were erected to accommodate the entire village and those from the nearby villages who had come to see the people who had been to another world.

The fetish priest entertained the people to some fine dancing and drumming. People talked and shared their views openly whilst others could be seen in groups gossiping about the missing people.

Suddenly, there was a vicious thunderstorm and rain began to pour. Out of curiosity, everyone stayed to witness the forthcoming event. Just after the rain had ceased, a very beautiful bird flew past the gathering and it was immediately recognised as the one that was picked up by the little girl at the riverside. Whilst all eyes were focused on the bird, there appeared from the bush Mr. Banquo, his three sons and Aisha. For once, silence engulfed the whole area. Fear gripped the villagers. "Are they ghosts or living beings?" they asked, but no one wanted to get close to them.

Suddenly the town crier picked up his gong-gong and started beating it harder than usual whilst shouting the homecoming of the missing people. The king was the first to embrace them, before all the villagers both young and old came to shake their hands and welcomed them. The whole village was filled with excitement and anxiety. The clothes that Mr Banquo and the children were dressed in were very expensive.

The villagers had never even dreamt of seeing clothing as rich and regal as what Mr Banquo and the children were wearing. One by one, the returnees narrated their experiences to the king and the gathering. In fact, as they narrated their adventure, the villagers felt as if they had been there themselves. It became the core of every conversation. The villagers and the chief himself were trying to touch their clothes to see if they too could be transferred to visit the other world.

Little Aisha had now gotten very used to Mr Banquo's family and considered herself as one of them.

CHAPTER 6

Mr Banquo seemed to have changed into a different person, as he was now very nice to the people. They could come to him freely with their problems and he was always willing to help.

A few months after their return, Mr Banquo's second son Kwabena fell in love and married Ama; the daughter of the fetish priest. She became pregnant but was always sick and the village doctor did not seem to find the cause of her illness. As Kwabena's circumstances did not allow him to have huge savings, he could not afford to take her to a specialist doctor in the city. He just thought it was probably the pregnancy that was making her ill, and left it to the village doctor.

The doctor mixed a potion for her to drink and immediately she felt fine, but later on, the pains became much more severe. Kwabena rushed her to the fetish priest who said River Selbs was responsible for her illness. "How so?" Kwabena asked. Then what the fetish priest said made Kwabena's jaw drop. He said the river lady loved Kwabena and did not want him to have anyone in his life apart from her. And although she felt this way, Kwabena did not know anything about her love for him.

Some rituals were performed and everything was back to normal until the time of the birth. Ama became restless and started screaming which brought most of the villagers running to Kwabena's house to see what was going on. The village doctor was called and upon examining her, he said she will deliver the baby in less than a week.

Four days after the doctor came to the house, another screaming was heard and again the villagers ran to Kwabena's house. Ama told them how she saw the lady from the River Selbs trying to take her unborn baby away from her. She also dreamt that before Kwabena could become free from the river lady, he would have to travel abroad to break the spell.

A week later, as the doctor said, Ama gave birth to a bouncing baby boy who they called Cudjoe. It was a very quick birth and she seemed fine after it. However, two days after the delivery, she complained of having a very bad headache. None of her family, including Kwabena took the headache seriously. They only offered her some herbal remedy with the hope that the headache would go away and it did. But that night, when she went to bed beside her baby, she never awoke the next morning. She was dead!

Chapter 7

This was a shock to the entire village and extremely painful for her family, not to mention Kwabena who was left with a two day old baby to care for. All he was left with now was the memory of his beautiful wife Ama. Poor Kwabena, though very sad, he endured as the days went by. He cared for his baby as any father should, although he himself was just a young man of seventeen.

Cudjoe was now one year old and growing into a big boy. He always made his dad laugh and he liked to be cuddled. Working on the farm and caring for Cudjoe was proving difficult for Kwabena. Then one day he remembered the dream his wife had about him travelling abroad.

Kwabena had no opportunity to go abroad. He remembered the good days with his wife; weeding the ground, planting the plantains, cocoyam, cassava, and peppers, which they sold at the market. He even shared his lunch on the farm, which was normally prepared by his wife. She was always in the kitchen at dawn, just as the rooster crowed. Kwabena fondly reminisced on the good life he had with his wife and he smiled.

Before he fell asleep he kept thinking and thinking, then all of a sudden a thought came to him. "I have to learn, I have to learn how to write and to speak English." Kwabena got up and went to his father's house and knocked. Mr Banquo who never experienced his son knocking on his door at that time of the morning shouted back to his son, "Come in Kwabena."

Kwabena went in and knelt in front of his father and said, "Papa I know money is very scarce but please can you let me attend school now before I grow too old. I promise I will continue helping you with the farm and you will never even notice that I have been missing." "Papa", Kwabena continued, "it would not be long before I will be reading your letters and you will not have to call the village teacher."

Mr Banquo woke up from the bed and asked his son to stand up. He said, "Kwabena you have almost grown past starting school, you have a child and none of the children at the school has a child, moreover the other children will be laughing at you. It will not be long before your son starts school with you." Kwabena replied to his father, "Daddy I know but I don't care what they say. If the village teacher will accept me, I will go."

Mr Banquo said to his son, "Kwabena, tomorrow, I will personally take you to the school and see the school teacher so that you can start as soon as possible." Kwabena was very happy. He went back to bed, but could not sleep until daybreak.

Mr Banquo took his son to the school and he was accepted. He started school and made friends. Kwabena could not play with them after school because he had grown past all his classmates. However he always returned to help his father at the farm, just as he had promised. He continued working on the farm. He grew increasingly sad and tearful as he missed his wife. However, that did not distract him from his education. As a matter of fact, he was even promoted twice to an upper class and eventually when he was in his last year at the school; he passed his exams with flying colours.

Kwabena's Agricultural Science teachers taught them a lot about agriculture and how good it was to grow one's own crops. This motivated Kwabena to stay on in the village and educate his father about farming and selling his crops. But most of his friends had left the village to go to the other cities and he wished to follow them.

As time went on, it became financially difficult for Kwabena to make a quick profit in the village, as the crops took a full year to grow before harvest time. So he thought he should take a break and leave the village for the city for a while. He discussed his intention with his elderly dad, who agreed. He left his son in the care of his dad with the help of his other siblings and their wives. Kwabena left for the city. He knew he would miss his family very much but he had to go to start his new life and also to try to forget about his sad past.

On arrival in the city, Kwabena rented himself a little room with the savings he had. After two weeks of searching for work, he found a job as a waiter in a restaurant, pretty close to his rented room. He was quite excited about this job. He believed this job would give him the opportunity to meet more people and take his mind off the sad past he left behind and hopefully help him to foster positive thinking. Little did Kwabena know what was in store for him.

One evening when Kwabena was smartly dressed up at work going about serving food to people, he served a man whose face looked familiar. He had a feeling that it was someone he knew from his childhood days in the village. However, he could not quite remember who this person was, as he was obviously now a grown man and quite bearded as well. Kwabena searched his memory, but no one came to mind. He was afraid to strike a conversation with the man, as he did not know how the man would react. Wanting to get on with his work he decided to push the thought behind him and carried on as normal. That night when he went home, Kwabena was quite restless and could not sleep. He could not help thinking that he knew the man he saw and blamed himself for not approaching him. He remembered the man was smartly dressed and spoke with that of a foreign accent. He tossed and turned so much in bed that night that he woke up very tired in the morning.

CHAPTER 8

That morning, as he was making himself breakfast, he suddenly had a flash back. He thought of Mama Akosua, an elderly woman from his village whom he knew as a child and whom he had not seen for many years. She became a bit of a recluse because of her many problems. Akosua had a grandson called Ezekiah whom Kwabena was friendly with as a child. Ezekiah's mother had died when he was quite young. As Kwabena and Ezekiah shared the same fate of growing up without a mother, they became quite close. They used to play together as children. But because Ezekiah was quite a troublesome boy, his grandmother, Akosua sent him to live with his uncle Mensah in the city. Kwabena and Ezekiah lost touch after he went; as Ezekiah never visited the village.

That night in his room Kwabena went deeper and deeper into his childhood memories, He reflected on his friendship with Ezekiah and he cherished the time they spent together as children. Even though he was still uncertain of the identity of the man, Kwabena promised himself that if he sees the man again, nothing would deter him from approaching him.

He went to work that day but the man did not show up at the restaurant. For weeks and months, he waited tirelessly to see the man but to no avail. Eventually Kwabena began to forget about the whole issue of ever seeing this man whom he thought could be Ezekiah.

Even though Kwabena rarely visited the village he always kept in touch by mail. He saved a large amount of money from his job, therefore without fail; he regularly posted money to his elderly dad to care for his family.

One day, after having been away for almost a year, Kwabena missed his family so much, he decided to pay them a surprise visit. Kwabena went shopping for almost the entire village. He bought shoes, shirts, and clothes for his brothers and their wives and food and toys for the children. His bags were so full that all eyes were on him at the bus station. Other passengers were annoyed that the bus journey was delayed as Kwabena had to pay extra to board the bus. He had so many bags.

Upon reaching the village, everyone warmly welcomed him and he felt at home.

Mr. Banquo, Josef, Kojo and Cudjoe were so happy to see Kwabena after so many months away. When Cudjoe saw his dad, he jumped on him and kissed him all over his face. Between the hugs and kisses, Cudjoe told Kwabena "Daddy, I love you and I missed you. Please take me to the city with you".

That broke Kwabena's heart and tears fell down his face as he hugged his little boy. Nevertheless, wanting to catch up on the occurrences in the village, he embraced his dad and both sat down on the veranda to catch up.

On hearing that Kwabena had arrived, the villagers queued to see him.

"Oh no, what am I going to do?" Kwabena pondered as the

villagers began to gather at the house, and little by little everyone got one of the goodies from Kwabena's bag.

Kwabena brought money and gifts for his family and friends in the village. Once the tears of joy of seeing his family was over, they chatted away into the night just as in the olden days. They watched people go past their home in the darkness of the night being guided only by the moon light. The little ones had gone off to sleep but Mr Banquo and Kwabena were too excited to sleep, they stayed awake all night.

Kwabena wanted to know who had died in the village, who got married, and who had migrated to a foreign country. Mr Banquo responded, "Oh my boy."

He then asked Kwabena if he remembered Mama Akosua. Kwabena paused for a while, and then responded with fright. "What a coincidence," he exclaimed. "Papa, it is funny you asked me, only the other day I thought of her!"

Now sitting on the edge of his chair, Kwabena asked, "Has she died?" Mr Banquo gave a hearty laugh and said "No son". "Mama Akosua is fine and still farming the land." "Do you know that Mama Akosua has a son in the city, called Kwesi?" Kwabena said yes. Mr Banquo continued, "Well my boy, he died of cancer two weeks ago and was brought here in the village to be buried on the family land." "Not only that, my boy," Mr Banquo said. "All the family came from foreign land, including Ezekiah, Mama Akosua's grandson. He came to ask of you." he went on.

At that point, Kwabena's eyes and mouth opened in

amazement. "My God!" he shouted. Standing to his feet, he asked his Dad, "Did you mean, Mama Akosua's grandson Ezekiah was here asking for me?" His dad asked him why he was so awed and Kwabena began to explain. "Dad, you will not believe this, but some months ago, in the restaurant where I worked, I saw a man who bore a striking resemblance to Ezekiah but I was afraid to approach him."

Mr Banquo said it could have been Ezekiah, as he went there ten months ago to see his sick uncle Kwesi who was hospitalized in the city. Kwabena put his face in his hands and his mind wandered off for a while. Seeing his despair, Mr Banquo said, "Never mind my boy, all is not lost, Ezekiah, came here asking for you again four days ago when he was on his way back to the city.

He said he had to return to the city to sort out his uncle's belongings but he would not be returning to the village though." Mr Banquo said that Ezekiah wanted to know how Kwabena was doing, and said if he had seen you now, he would never recognize you.

"Here," Mr Banquo said, handing Kwabena a piece of paper, "Ezekiah left you this note". Kwabena could not believe his eyes. He opened the note with shaking hands, eager to see what was written on the paper. The note bore the address and telephone number of Ezekiah, and asked Kwabena to give him a call on the foreign numbers in two weeks, as he was soon returning to Canada. Kwabena said to himself "Well all is not lost; at least I have an address from him?"

CHAPTER 9

Kwabena was now filled with excitement and couldn't wait to go back to the city for work, hoping that Ezekiah would visit the restaurant again. Well Kwabena said to his dad "it is going to be a long day tomorrow. I must get some rest now because I have to be up early in the morning to see my friends before leaving for the city."

When morning came, Mr Banquo prepared a big and healthy breakfast of tilapia (a tropical fish) and okro stew with banku (corn dough mixed with cassava dough) for Kwabena. Kwabena enjoyed the delicious breakfast prepared by his dad and that brought more memories back.

He later went out to see his friends, deliver gifts, and catch up on the current gossip. He also visited relatives who were excited to see him. He returned home late that evening and spent the rest of the evening with his dad. As they sat together, he comforted his son Cudjoe.

The next morning Kwabena left for the city. Mr Banquo and Cudjoe begged him to come back soon and reminded him to call Ezekiah. On his journey back, he could not stop thinking about the coincidence of Ezekiah also looking for him, so he prayed to God that he would see Ezekiah before his return to Canada.

The next day after he got back to the city, Kwabena went to work very early in the morning to carry on his duty as a waiter. He took gifts consisting of coconut, mangos, guavas and coco yams (a type of yam) to his boss. Days went by but there was no sign of the man he thought to be Ezekiah.

One day, Kwabena was asked to work in the kitchen to prepare the meals as one of his work colleagues was sick and did not come to work.

Kwabena was not happy with this request because he believed if the man he thought was Ezekiah came, he would once again miss another opportunity to meet him. Kwabena thought perhaps with the gifts he brought from the village to his boss, he could now ask back a favour from him. He asked if another colleague could be at the back in order for him to be at the front. His boss would not have any of that and became annoyed when Kwabena mentioned the gift. He asked if he was blackmailing him and eventually Kwabena had no choice but to do as requested in order to keep his job. While working that day, he was sure to occasionally visit the eating area.

When he had some free time he helped to pick up the eating trays from the table. Little did Kwabena know that luck would come his way that day. Whilst picking up the trays at the far corner of the restaurant, he noticed a man sitting on his own. He went nearer to the table to have a closer look. It was the same man he had seen 10 months ago. He could not contain himself. He knew it was now or never. He quickly brought his trays to the kitchen and asked his boss if he could have his break, since it was now less busy. His boss said yes.

Kwabena mustered courage and went up to the table and greeted the man. The man looked up and said, "Hello."

Nervously, Kwabena asked, "Are you Ezekiah?" He stared fixedly at Kwabena, and then answered "yes" in a nice calm voice. The man removed his glasses, looked closer, and asked, "Who are you?"

Kwabena replied, "I am Kwabena, Mr. Banquo's son," The man shouted, "Kwabena! Do you mean my childhood friend Kwabena?" Kwabena nodded yes. Ezekiah shook his head and said, "My God! You have changed!" "I could not even recognize you."

Kwabena said the same to Ezekiah. He explained to him that he saw him in the restaurant ten months ago and thought he knew him but for some reason was afraid to approach him.

At that point Ezekiah explained that he did visit some time ago, when he came to see his uncle in the hospital. He also told Kwabena that he only just returned from the village again and this time he left an address with his dad for him. Kwabena told him that he knew, as he had only just returned from the village some days ago as well. "My dad told me everything and gave me your address," said Kwabena.

The two men were so excited to see each other and to finally meet again after many years. They hugged and chatted for a while, eager to catch up on the past. Unfortunately, as time went by, Kwabena was reminded by his boss that his lunch break was over. The restaurant was beginning to get busy again. As Kwabena was about to break up with his friend, his boss Mr Appiah, approached and introduced himself to Ezekiah. He asked Kwabena why he did not inform him about his friend visiting, as he could have arranged a longer break for him. But both Ezekiah and Kwabena shook their heads smiling, as they were not expecting each other.

Kwabena then told his boss all that happened and how he was praying to see his friend again. The boss laughed and asked Kwabena to spend as much time with his friend. He jokingly reminded him that this will cost him a double share of fruits next time, if he was expected to do his job while he chatted. Ezekiah gave Kwabena some money, and reminded him to call, since he was leaving for Canada that night. They embraced each other, shook hands and soon, Kwabena returned to work.

Ezekiah thanked Kwabena's boss, who asked him a few questions about Canada; the life, the people and the food. As Ezekiah was describing life over there to Mr Appiah, he became jealous and started dreaming of selling his restaurant and migrating. Apparently he forgot he was helping Kwabena with some of the work, as all of a sudden the restaurant became crowded.

Thinking aloud Mr Appiah shouted, "I am going to Canada, I am going to sell my restaurant!" With all the customers suddenly laughing and shaking their heads, Mr Appiah realised how loud he had spoken.

Ezekiah left for Canada and Kwabena continued working to save money. He was hoping for a better life and to provide for the needs of his family.

CHAPTER 10

Soon enough, it was now five months since Kwabena met with his friend, Ezekiah. Within those five months, Kwabena attempted to call him in Canada but his phone rung without answer, so he was unable to leave a message.

One day after a hard day at work, he went home to find he had got mail. When he picked it up from the door, the return address was from Ezekiah. Kwabena anxiously and happily opened his mail and read the contents with wide eyes. He read the lines repeatedly. Half way through the mail, he could not believe what good fortune was to come his way. Ezekiah was inviting him for a visit to Canada and said he would help him to pay his fare. As he read further down the letter, Ezekiah asked him to call on a new number as his previous number was changed. He was asked to call to confirm his acceptance of this visit.

After finishing work that evening, Kwabena, without hesitation, went directly to the pay phone box and called Ezekiah. He told him he got his letter and was accepting the offer to visit Canada. Ezekiah was happy to hear from him. He gave him all the instructions to apply for the visa at the Canadian Embassy.

Two weeks later, Kwabena applied and was granted a one-year visitor's visa to Canada. He was so excited. He danced around his room for a while and went and called Ezekiah immediately to give him the good news. Oh how happy Ezekiah was for his friend and told him he was looking forward to receive him into his home.

Kwabena thought of writing to his father about the good news, but thinking of it carefully, he changed his mind and rather decided to visit him in person.

Kwabena also shared the good news with his boss and expressed his wish to visit Canada in the coming month. His boss was not able to keep the post open until his return, so Kwabena had to resign from his job.

Hearing from his boss that his job could not be guaranteed for him to come back to, Kwabena realised that his boss was not sorry to let him go.

Surely, Kwabena thought "I would come back to this restaurant one day, not to serve, but to be served." Kwabena then burst into a very loud laughter, patted his boss on his shoulder and said, "Boss, don't worry, I'll be back, and who knows, I might help you to make this restaurant one of the biggest and most famous in the city."

Kwabena then paid a surprise visit to his village once again. Hearing the news about Kwabena's short visit, his father was not only surprised, but also afraid something might have happened as Kwabena just left the village a few weeks ago. As almost all the villagers gathered to hear what brought Kwabena back so soon, the father sat down with some elders as was their tradition and water was brought. Kwabena drank some then poured the remaining on the ground for the gods, as was their custom.

After Kwabena greeted the elders, he was asked the reason for the unusually short interval between the last visit and this. He took his time, breathed in and out, took a very, very close look at the elders, then looked at the crowd, stood up, stretched his arms then shouted to the crowd, "I am going overseas. I am going to the white man's country. I am going to sit in the plane." On hearing that, Kwabena's father stood up, held him, carried him high, and joined him shouting with joy.

Mr Banquo then ordered his biggest goat be slaughtered and asked the villagers to join them that night in celebration. The villagers played their local drums and it continued till the early hours of the next morning.

Kwabena was happy to be leaving for Canada, but sad to leave Cudjoe and his dad behind. His dad strengthened him by giving words of encouragement and reassuring him that he would not let anything happen to Cudjoe. On the day Kwabena boarded the bus back to the city, tears were flowing down his cheeks, as there was no guarantee how soon he would see them again. His family as well as the villagers were also crying.

When the day arrived for Kwabena to travel to the airport, he carried two old suitcases and two sack bags. The suitcases contained some African clothes, sandals, shirts and pairs of traditional shorts. The sack bags contained herbs, traditional medicine, local gin, some tropical fried fish and prepared food. At the airport check in, one of the attendants explained to Kwabena that he wouldn't need all of those cotton shirts and shorts as the weather will be cold on his arrival. Moreover, she told him they might not allow him to carry all of those things as his luggage was overweight. Eventually, Kwabena took some of his clothes out from the suitcases as he was advised. He removed his short-sleeved shirt and put on a long-sleeved one instead, with his jacket on top.

Although he was already forewarned about the conditions of winter in Canada, nothing could have prepared Kwabena for the weather.

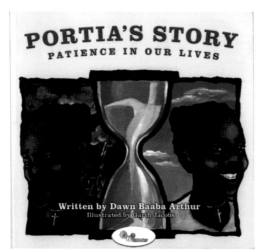

ALSO BY DAWN B. ARTHUR

PORTIA'S STORY:

PATIENCE IN OUR LIVES

Portia's Story is a modern fairy tale of a woman who has everything she has ever dreamed of, but loses it all after her husband dies. After burying her husband, his family wastes no time in telling Portia and her three children to vacate farm on which the house was is built because they own it. Portia then has to work her way out of this situation. The story stays faithful to the genre, with a benefactor wanting nothing in return for his help and the eventual rise of the downtrodden Portia from adversity to strength and success, without losing her humanity in the process. Most of all, **Portia's Story** is about using what happens to you as an inspiration to become a better person or to preserve the good character you have. Set in a fictional place in Ghana, and aimed at 7 - 10 year olds, **Portia's Story** illustrates the principles of forgiveness, patience, faith, hard work and turning set-backs into opportunities for personal growth and change. It is also about following your heart and doing what needs to be done to make your dreams real.

A lot of younger people today aspire to the celebrity lifestyles so often portrayed in music videos and magazines, with little consideration for what it truly takes to reach those dizzying heights of success or stardom. Reading **Portia's Story** can help to shed light on what it is like to have everything, lose it and regain it, accepting help where it is offered along the way and learning the meaning of true friendship and trust.

ALBUMS BY
DAWN B. ARTHUR

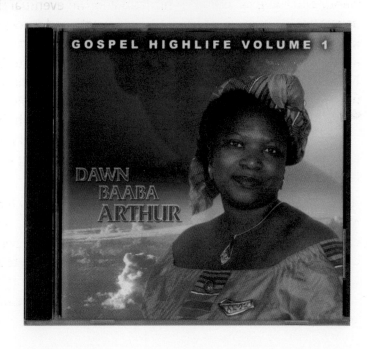

ALSO BY DAWN B. ARTHUR

TILL I CAN DO NO MORE
A BOOK OF POEMS